Flamingo *Feet*

Written by:

Shreya Gupta

Tellwell Talent
www.tellwell.ca

ISBN
978-0-2288-3347-5 (Hardcover)
978-0-2288-3346-8 (Paperback)

Dedicated to my loving parents, who taught
me to always believe in myself.

And to all young girls who have a dream—never give up on yourself.

Aria dreamed of being a dancer when she grew up. She particularly liked jazz dancing, and she was a natural at it. Aria wasn't taking lessons, but there was a dance studio across the street.

"Mom, can we go to the dance studio?" asked Aria one Saturday morning. "There's a competition I want to enter!"

"Will they let you enter if you don't take lessons there?" her mom asked.

"I saw other kids going to enter who don't go there," Aria replied.

"Very well then, honey, let's go."

When they entered the studio, Aria felt very excited. She had never seen so many people dancing in one room before! While Aria's mom talked to a teacher, Aria ran over to the sign-up sheet. She was about to write her name when suddenly some kids came up to her that she knew from school.

"Hey, we've seen you dance before!" said one of the kids. "You're terrible!"

"When have you seen me dance?" asked Aria.

"How do you NOT know?" asked another kid in the group. "You tell everyone to watch you dance and then you just trip! HAHA! Your name should be Flamingo Feet. HAHA!"

"I don't have flamingo feet!" exclaimed Aria. "I just fall because I get nervous. I don't mean to!"

"Like we care!" someone else replied. Then they all laughed and walked away.

Aria was now very hurt. It wasn't her fault she got nervous sometimes. Her mom said it was just stage fright. Aria wasn't going to let some mean bullies crush her dream, so she scribbled her name on the sign-up sheet.

She had one week before the rehearsal for the competition, so Aria practiced at home every night. She was so excited.

The day finally came for the rehearsal. Aria was a little nervous when she entered the studio, but she tried to reassure herself that everything would be okay.

"Came back to try and make a fool of yourself?" teased one of the bullies.

"As a matter of fact, I've come to win first place!" Aria replied.

"Good luck, Flamingo Feet. HAHA!" replied the bully.

Aria was starting to feel more nervous. It looked like most of the kids who took lessons at the dance studio were at the rehearsal.

"It's okay," Aria whispered to herself, "all you have to do is practice the jazz moves you're going to perform. It's okay."

Aria found an open spot on the floor. She practiced her moves but got too nervous and fell. She got back up and tried again but the same thing happened.

"Hey, Flamingo Feet, why are you falling? Is your one leg not working for you?!" laughed the bully.

"I have two feet and I'm not a flamingo!" Aria yelled.

When the other kids heard the bully calling Aria "Flamingo Feet" some of them did too.

"Flamingo Feet! Flamingo Feet!" the kids yelled.

Aria ran out of the room and crossed her name off the list. She no longer wanted to be in the competition. As she was heading for the doors with tears in her eyes, she saw a little girl sitting alone on a bench.

"Why are you sitting out here by yourself?" Aria asked.

"I'm waiting for my mommy to pick me up," said the girl. "Why do you look like you just got kicked in the face?"

"Oh! Umm ... I was in rehearsal for the competition, and I kept falling because I have stage fright. Everyone was calling me Flamingo Feet, so I left and dropped out of the competition."

"That's why you're sad?" asked the little girl. "OH! Well, I used to be called Butter Toes, but I didn't let that stop me."

"What do you mean?" Aria asked.

"Don't let anyone stop you from chasing your dreams," said the little girl. "Be who you want to be—no matter what anyone says. Here, this is my good luck charm."

The little girl unclipped a ballerina pin from her shirt and handed it to Aria.

"I take this with me wherever I go," explained the little girl, "but I think you need it more than me."

"Thank you, kid," said Aria. "Sadly, the world is not that simple."

Aria walked away with the charm in her hand. She had a good, yet strange feeling about the charm. Her mom was waiting for her outside the studio.

"How did it go?" asked Aria's mother.

"It went well," lied Aria. "I don't really want to talk about it right now."

"Ok, honey," said Aria's mom.

Thoughts of the dance competition haunted Aria all night. She tossed and turned and finally fell asleep very late into the night.

The next morning, Aria woke up determined. She wanted to sign up again for the dance competition. There was just one problem: it was too late to sign up now.

"What will I do?" Aria asked herself. She decided to ask her mom to take her to the dance studio again.

"Why, honey?" asked Aria's mom. "You already signed up and rehearsals are now done!"

"Well ... I kind of ... dropped out of the competition," Aria reluctantly admitted.

"Honey, why in the world would you do that?" exclaimed her mom.

"I don't really want to talk about it right now. I do want to sign up again though."

"Okay, well tell me when you are ready, honey. I'm proud of you for not giving up!"

Once Aria and her mom arrived at the dance studio, Aria's mom went to talk to one of the dance teachers to hear details about the competition. Aria went to talk to Mrs. Weller, the head of the studio.

"Hi, Mrs. Weller!" exclaimed Aria. "I dropped out of the competition, but I really want to sign up once more. I know the sign-up dates are over, but I was getting bullied and that's why I dropped out. Please, please, please give me another chance!"

"Fine," said Mrs. Weller. "Only this one time."

Aria was excitedly walking down the hall to the sign-up sheet when she saw the bullies again.

"Heeeyyyy, Flamingo Feet!" laughed the bullies.

"You've come back to fall on your face, I see," said one of the bullies.

Aria was very hurt, but she clutched the good luck charm the little girl had given her. Holding it in her hand, she felt very confident and said, "Back off! I don't care what you say about me—I'm fulfilling my dream!"

The bullies looked surprised. They didn't seem to know what to say. Aria walked confidently past the bullies and put her name on the sign-up sheet.

The competition was in two days. Those two days seemed like forever to Aria, but the competition day finally arrived.

Aria arrived at the studio in her favourite dress. She felt beautiful. When it was her turn to go, Aria saw her mom in the audience with her thumbs up and smiling. Aria started with a twirl, but she tripped because of her stage fright. She heard whispers of "Flamingo Feet" in the audience and some giggles. Aria clenched the good luck charm and got back up.

"The charm will help me," whispered Aria to herself.

Aria then started to dance. She did a variety of different jazz moves including a pivot turn, a pirouette and a split leap. The audience was very quiet. Aria began to worry that no one was liking her performance.

She clenched the good luck charm and danced even more, improvising different and new moves into her dance routine. Once she was finished, the audience went wild and started cheering. Aria got a standing ovation for her performance. She was in total shock.

At the end of the competition, they announced the winner. To Aria's surprise, she won first place! She went backstage with tears of joy and saw her mom.

"Mommy, look!" cried Aria. "My good luck charm worked!"

Aria's mom gave her a big hug and congratulated her for the amazing performance and winning the competition.

"Honey, where did you get that good luck charm?" asked Aria's mom.

"It's a long story, but it's the reason I won!" said Aria.

"Are you sure about that?" asked her mother.

Aria was confused. What did her mother mean? Then she suddenly realized that the only thing she needed was confidence all along. Everything that happened during her performance came from within herself.

Aria opened her hand and stared at the good luck charm. She smiled down at the ballerina pin and realized the pin had nothing to do with her winning the competition. She skipped confidently out of the dance studio knowing that she would never doubt herself again.

About the Author

Shreya Gupta raises money for various charities that help young girls access education in third-world countries. Her goal is to inspire young girls around the world to always chase their dreams, no matter what. In her spare time, Shreya enjoys sketching, reading and writing stories, of course! She takes jazz dancing lessons too, which inspired her to write this book about a girl's dream to jazz dance.

CPSIA information can be obtained at www.ICGtesting.com
Printed in the USA
LVIW011932300720
661974LV00007B/40